THE BLUNDERING BILLIONAIRE

CHACE VERITY

THE BLUNDERING BILLIONAIRE

Chace Verity

The Blundering Billionaire originally appeared in the anthology *Rogue Ever After* (2019).

For Corey

Thank you for liking my Courtney Milan joke—that was the most meaningful praise I had ever received from you about one of my books. I didn't know it would be the last. I miss you.

ONE

Millions of people around the world bought coffee every day. The task of purchasing a beverage surely came as easy as breathing to most people. Jayden-James Hancock, however, was not most people, and he wanted to sink into the earth when the bastion of caffeinated options greeted him during his first trip inside a coffee shop.

If only Jay knew what his old assistant used to order for him. Jay craved that sweet drink. What the hell was it?! Caramel, soy, espresso, Colombian? Why did the menu have so many words?

The shop itself was bereft of people save for a lone customer in the corner. The Monahan's barista must have been in the back, leaving the flustered 32-year-old without anyone to consult for advice.

Jay turned to his phone. As embarrassing as it

would be to admit to his thirty million SuddenPic followers he had never been inside a coffee shop before, he could crowdsource them for recommendations. His followers always had suggestions for restaurants and hotels, though it was his assistant who set the itineraries.

Or used to, anyway.

Losing his assistant had been devastating, but Jay hadn't thought twice about firing Caleb after discovering his disgusting secret. Caleb had sold numerous risqué images of Jay's half-sister to tabloid magazines. Jay wasn't a particularly useful part of the Hancock-Strauss family, but he was good at being a big brother.

"Excuse me!"

Jay glanced up to meet the eager, sweet voice's owner.

The woman greeting him had six or so inches over him. The first thing Jay noticed in people was their height. At 5'2", most everyone towered over him. His supermodel sisters, having been blessed with height from their skyscraper-shaped father, were giants compared to him. Lifts could only give Jay a couple of inches before he started tripping over his shadow.

The woman held a sheet of paper in her hands. "Do you have a pen I could borrow? Mine just died."

Ah. The customer in the corner. An autograph seeker, no doubt.

He soaked in the rest of the woman as he fished out his pen. She was as cute as her voice—round, rosy, freckled cheeks and big, plump lips as pink as her parka jacket. The jacket didn't pair well with her frizzy red hair she had pinned in a bun, but it highlighted her soft, earthy brown eyes.

His gaze flicked down to the rest of her. Jeggings were the bane of his family's existence, but he liked the way this pair hugged the woman's curves. Jay didn't recognize the brand of her running shoes, but their worn out condition suggested this woman valued comfort over appearance.

That wasn't a bad quality to have.

Jay held the pen, waiting to sign her paper. He was curious what kind of name this bubbly lady possessed.

The woman took the pen. "Thank you! I'll bring it right back."

Jay kept his hand positioned to sign an autograph, despite no longer having a writing utensil. "Huh?"

She dashed off to her corner of the coffee shop, leaving Jay to nurse his confused, bruised ego. Did she not recognize him?

It wasn't that Jay *wanted* to be recognized by the masses. After a lifetime in the limelight, though, he expected it. He grew up being photographed. Even for a simple thing like coffee, Jay had to dress his best. Today's outfit involved an oversized scarf and a slim, navy wool suit embroidered with golden flowers.

Jay took another gander at Monahan's menu. Not like coffee was simple.

With no sign of the barista, still, Jay drew in a large breath and approached the pen-borrower. "Excuse me."

Her gaze shot straight up. "Oh, do you need your pen? I'm almost done! Please let me have another minute."

"Oh, uh, it's okay." Jay scratched the back of his neck. "That's not what I wanted to ask. I was wondering if you would tell me what you're drinking? I don't know what to order."

The woman broke into a relieved smile. Her increased adorableness caused Jay's pulse to flutter.

"It's a butterscotch cappuccino with two shots of espresso. It's so good, especially if you get whipped cream on it! I almost never get to order it, but I treated myself today since I'm putting in fifty applications." The woman blushed and turned back to her paper. "I might be feeling the espresso. I'm not usually this loud."

Jay worked his jaw. He wanted to laugh, but he worried she would misconstrue it as him mocking her. For whatever few seconds he could be in this lovely woman's presence, he wanted to leave a good impression. "I'll order one of those. When does the barista come back?"

"You have to ring the bell." The woman pointed to the counter. "She's doing inventory. Gosh, I might be a barista the next time you come here."

"This is a job application?" Jay craned his head to the side. He had never seen one before. Resumes and CVs, sure, but a form asking about useless stuff like high school diplomas? It was interesting to take a gander at how most people found gainful employment.

"It'd be awesome to work here, wouldn't it?" The woman grinned at him. "Imagine all the discounted coffee I could get."

Speaking of... He really needed to order before the caffeine headache arrived.

God. Ordering coffee. Alone.

His mother's secretary had offered to hire someone for him. Anybody Noreen hired would have been an excellent replacement for Caleb, but it was difficult for Jay to explain his hesitancy. An assistant was a trusted member of the family. Caleb had violated that trust.

Hopefully the job-seeker's recommendation

would suit his tastes so he didn't have to worry about trying something else.

The barista came out and took Jay's order. Minutes later, after struggling to remember his debit card's PIN and taking a selfie with the barista who *did* recognize him, Jay finally had his caffeinated beverage.

Jay fixed his gaze on the job-seeker in the corner while he took a sip. The drink was as sweet as he wanted. Not what Caleb used to order for him, but Jay could get used to this.

The woman scrambled from the table. "Thank you! I'm all done."

Jay watched her as she set the application on the counter. Wisps of escaped hair curled around her ears. Everything about her screamed vibrant and wholesome.

It would be a mistake to never see her again.

Maybe she would like dinner in Milan next Friday night? If Jay could figure out how to buy a plane ticket for her.

"Do you like your cappuccino?" asked the woman.

"Yes, thank you." Jay gestured for her to keep the pen. "Are you good at other, uh, decisions?"

Jay groaned internally as the question fumbled passed his lips. His romantic encounters with people had never started with any semblance of grace. For all the money and status available to him, he couldn't buy confidence.

"I suppose I am." The woman held out her phone. She had it opened to a notes application, filled with a list of places. "These are all the places I'm going to apply to. I've written out why I like each of these places, in case I get an on-the-spot interview."

Jay peered at the screen over the rim of his round spectacles. Her attention to detail was interesting. She had the places listed geographically and ranked them by which job she wanted the most. Monahan's had the coveted number one spot.

"Are you always like this?" Jay asked. "Organized?"

The woman nodded. "I have to be. I have a lot of medication to take and bills to pay. It's important to get a job today."

Determined people had always caused sparks to fly in Jay's chest—sparks no amount of money could ever buy. These sparks often turned Jay's brain off and made him more impulsive. No less clumsy, of course, but certainly more proactive.

She reached for the bell, but Jay blocked her hand.

He took the application from the counter. "Do you like Milan, Miss Dyer?"

Isla Dyer. What a gorgeous name.

She blinked. "Milan? Like Courtney Milan? Yes, I do."

"Er, I meant Italy. I have to go there for a conference next Friday." Jay folded the application in half and took a deep breath. "Perhaps you would like to come with me?"

"Why?" Isla's brow wrinkled with concern.

Jay's nerves bloomed to newfound heights, and it had nothing to do with the two shots of espresso. "I'm not a serial killer, if that's what you're thinking! I'm Jayden-James Hancock. Like, you know, from Hancock-Strauss."

"So you're a businessman?" Isla's frown deepened. "Serial killers can be businessmen, too, for your information."

Jay bit his lower lip to stifle his laughter. Did she really not recognize him? "I'm more of a professional son."

Before he could press on with this awkward attempt at securing a date, Isla gasped and brought her hands to her cheeks. Her cute, surprised pose made him forget what words even were.

"Are you offering me a job?" she asked. "Like you need an assistant?"

That...wasn't entirely inaccurate. Jay *did* need a new assistant.

He clenched his jaw. If this lovely, sweet person

didn't know Jay or his family, that meant her impression of him hinged only on this cringe-worthy encounter. Who would be interested in a short, socially awkward man that got overwhelmed by a coffee shop menu?

Perhaps the only reasonable way to continue spending time with Isla would be through a business arrangement.

However, did he trust her to be his assistant? She could pick a delicious beverage, but one conversation wasn't enough to instill the trust Jay required.

Jay kept his gaze on her. The hope shining in Isla's stunning eyes made him *want* to trust her.

"Yes." Jay tucked Isla's application into his coat pocket. "I'm offering you a job."

ISLA DYER WAS USED TO GOING TO WORK. SHE wasn't used to work coming to her.

A tanned woman with long, ebony black hair had shown up at Isla's horrifically messy apartment before dawn, armed with a metallic briefcase. Gold chains sparkled like constellations around the woman's neck. She introduced herself as Noreen, the Hancock-Strauss family secretary.

Isla gaped at the clean, stunning woman as

Noreen opened the briefcase. How could anyone be so well put together at five in the morning? Isla wasn't often conscious of her clothes, but her off-white flannel pajamas certainly paled in comparison to Noreen's sleek hot pink suit.

"Do you, uh, want any coffee?" Isla winced as she asked the question. Instant coffee was the only kind they had in this duct-tape-covering-holes apartment, and it wasn't even hers to offer. Garrett might be irate if he found out his powdered manna had been taken without permission when he woke up.

Neither of her roommates had believed her last night when she told them about her new job. Would they believe it if they saw Noreen and her gem-studded high heels in their kitchen?

Truthfully, Isla had scarcely believed it herself when she searched Jayden-James Hancock on the internet and got 220,000,000 hits.

"Thank you, but I prefer we get right to business." Noreen handed an expensive-looking platinum rectangle to Isla. "This is the tablet you'll be using to make Jayden-James's daily itinerary. I input the family's schedules into the cloud, and it automatically populates on the calendar app. It will be your responsibility to organize those schedules plus any appointments Jayden-James privately makes.

It is also your responsibility to ensure he gets from point A to point B."

Isla nodded, fighting back a yawn. Would she have to get up this early every day? She had turned into a night owl since getting laid off from the bookstore three months ago. She picked up a few hours here and there at gay clubs as a barback, but the gigs were notoriously unreliable.

Curiously, before she came out as trans, she never had a hard time finding work as a barback.

Isla unlocked the tablet as soon as Noreen gave her the password.

An article about the Hancock-Strauss spring show flashed across the screen. Fashion magnate Dee Hancock appeared in the photos with her children, decked in her signature violet sunglasses. The sixty-year-old with a short crop and rich, dark brown skin looked like she belonged in a spy movie.

Isla's gaze roved to the lone man in the picture. Where everyone else in the group photo stared directly at the camera, daring the world to challenge them, the lean, handsome man with light brown skin and black twists swept to the side studied his sleeve. His large, dark eyes couldn't be seen well in this particular photo, nor in any of the millions of images available on the internet.

Isla had enjoyed looking at photos of her future boss last night.

Noreen held up a platinum smartphone. "This is the phone you will use for business. It has all of Jayden-James's business contacts, including my number if you have questions. You will also use this to pay for all of Jayden-James's expenses."

"Pay?" Isla blinked.

"There's a credit card linked to this phone. You tap the phone's screen on the point of sale terminal. The device has face recognition, meaning you will be the only person who can access the phone." Noreen set the phone down on the kitchen counter.

Isla furrowed her brow. She knew about contactless payments, but she had never done it herself. Most places she visited barely had machines that could read chips in cards. Was she even qualified for this job? "What if we go somewhere that doesn't accept credit cards in a phone?"

Noreen returned Isla's frown. "Why would you go somewhere like that?"

Oh.

Noreen dangled a white card attached to a violet lanyard. "This is your key to the Hancock-Strauss complex. You only need to swipe it in front of the RFID readers. As Jayden-James's assistant, you have the same access as him. As the guards get to know you, they'll let you in automatically, but I still recommend carrying the ID badge at all times."

Isla admired the piece of plastic. The badge already had her photo and name on it. "Where did you find this photo?"

"Jayden-James scoped out your SuddenPic." Noreen shrugged. "He liked this picture the best."

Panic froze Isla in place. Jayden-James had looked at her SuddenPic profile!? 20% of her SuddenPic talked about incredibly vulnerable gender feelings and difficulties with being a broke trans woman. The other 80% SuddenPic revolved around student loan reformation rallies and petitions.

Isla wasn't ashamed about her involvement in student loan reformation. Far from it. No one deserved to be trapped in interest rates they could never hope to pay back before retirement if they wanted to pursue higher education.

It just seemed weird for a freaking billionaire to know about her struggles to pay $300 a month. Especially when Isla never got to put her communications degree to use.

Isla looped the lanyard around her fingers. "My SuddenPic profile isn't all I am, you know."

Noreen nodded. "Jayden-James agrees with that statement. He said he figured out everything he needed to know when you talked yesterday. He says you're nice, helpful, organized, and determined."

He...

He said all that?

Noreen continued. "The passcode to Jayden-James's private residence is 0712. He lives with the rest of the family in the Hancock-Strauss condo, but he has a separate elevator to his floor. You'll probably have to wake him up personally." Noreen set a bag of key fobs down. "These are backups to Jayden-James's cars. Each one is labeled. Sometimes he gets drunk and needs someone to drive his car home. Not just anyone can be trusted to drive one of his vehicles. There might be sensitive material in the backseat, like an unreleased prototype of a new purse, or Jayden-James might simply have a guest we wish to keep out of the public eye."

Isla gulped. Would she have to drive a freaking Lamborghini sometime?

Jealousy slowly crept in her stomach as the implication of Noreen's words sunk in. Would she have to chauffeur Jayden-James while he had sloppy make-out sessions with someone?!

Isla willed her stomach to get it under control. That was fine. Taxi drivers all over the world dealt with drunk kissy faces every day. Jayden-James was allowed to mack with whoever he wanted.

He was her boss. He was a means to a steady paycheck. Nothing else. Her student loan interest had ballooned out of control, hormones weren't free, and rent in New York City proved prohibitively expensive even with two roommates.

Stable income. If Isla could secure a job with a steady paycheck that left her enough cash to eat something besides peanut butter sandwiches, she'd be set. At twenty-seven, she feared the rest of her life would be a continuous scramble for security. She had never known anything else.

Isla ran her hands through her uncombed hair. God, she wished she had had some notice about Noreen's visit. The stylish secretary probably didn't think much of this unkempt ginger. "Can I ask how much my pay is?"

"That's a fair question." Noreen took out a document. "I'll need you to sign here, anyway, and give some more information I couldn't procure online."

Yikes. What else did Noreen and Jayden-James know about her? Isla didn't have sinister secrets, but it embarrassed her to consider the possibility they had dug up her medical history or *Kingdom Hearts* fanfic.

Noreen handed the document over. Isla read the thin sheet of paper carefully. If any part of this night owl was still asleep, that changed when she saw the number of zeroes on the paper.

"You'll admittedly be paid a little less than the rest of the assistants the family employs," Noreen said. "Given your lack of experience as a personal assistant, it's a good starting place. We can renegotiate in the future after your six month probation period is up. You'll have insurance and your travel expenses covered. As you know, we have a trip to Milan coming up next week."

A good starting place? This was a fabulous ending place! Isla could pay off her student loans in a few years, pay her mother back for all the emergency loans, never worry about getting hormones, *and* she could start a savings account.

Plus she would get to go to *Italy*!

Every inch of Isla's skin tingled in disbelief. There was no way she was actually qualified for this job in the first place.

"Thank you," Isla eked. "Do we need to wrap this up soon? I imagine you came over early because Mr. Hancock has a busy schedule. Do I have time to shower before I start working? I'm kind of a sweaty mess right now, as you can tell."

A smirk unfurled across Noreen's pretty face. "You have plenty of time. Thank you for letting me visit you. It's been interesting getting to know you."

Not like I had a choice.

"You have a communications degree, correct?" Noreen suddenly asked.

"I do," Isla answered. She paused. "Why?"

Noreen removed a gold-plated pen from her pocket. "Finally getting a chance to put it to use, huh? Makes the student loans a little less bitter, doesn't it? Maybe you won't need to attend protests and rallies so much now."

Isla's heart clanged against her chest.

Was her passion for student loan reformation going to be a problem?

TWO

JAY COVERED HIS HEAD WITH A PILLOW AS THE BELL rang for the fifth time. Who dared to bother him so early in the morning with that infernal bing-bong-bing? If it was one of his sisters, they could just walk right in, like they always did. As would his mother and stepfather.

He jumped out of bed, realizing that there was only one person who wouldn't just walk right in.

His new assistant. Oh, no.

Jay checked himself in the mirror while removing his satin scarf. No morning wood. No eyeliner smeared across the side of his face. No stains on his shirt from last night's two AM taco delivery while he got lost in the amazing world of *Kingdom Hearts III*.

He grimaced. Why did he care about his appearance? He had to squash this crush.

Jay dashed to the door before the bell rang for the sixth time.

Isla's bubbly smile sparkled like a star cutting through the night sky. Her cheeks were a marvelous shade of pink, enhancing every speck of her shining eyes. She smelled like a heavenly blend of lavender and coffee.

Coffee!

Isla held the to-go cup out to him. "Good morning, Mr. Hancock! I did some research on the tablet your mom's secretary gave me, and I found receipts for this drink. This is your favorite kind of coffee, right? Vanilla chai macchiato with almond milk."

Is that what Caleb used to get Jay? Jay sampled the drink.

The instant familiarity of the first sweet sip rubbed salt in Jay's wounded heart. Yes, this was what Caleb used to get.

The fact Isla had figured it out so quickly impressed Jay, but the drink tasted too much like Caleb now. Too much like betrayal.

"Thank you." Jay waved Isla inside. She had a black messenger bag covered in a rainbow of buttons. It suited her. "I, uh, like what you suggested for me the other day more. Could we start our days off with that instead?"

Isla had truly mastered the art of dropping her jaw in surprise. When caught off-guard, her mouth morphed into a heart.

So cute.

"Of course, Mr. Hancock!" Isla pulled a tablet out from her bag once they got to the living room. "I'll make a note. One butterscotch cappuccino with two shots of espresso and whipped cream on top every day."

"Two." Jay took another sip and studied Isla. She was even taller than him now since he was barefoot and she had donned a pair of black high heels. Admittedly, this fact was a bit titillating. "You said it's your favorite, right?"

Isla bit her lower lip as she nodded, tapping away at the screen.

God, he could stare at her mouth all day.

"Oh!" Isla pointed to the coffee table in front of the television. It was covered in taco wrappers and empty soda cans.

Ugh. He would have cleaned up if he had known Isla would be here.

"Are you playing *Kingdom Hearts III*?" Isla smiled. "I love that series. I can't afford to get the new game, but I've been watching some livestreams. It's amazing, isn't it?"

Wait, wait, wait. Isla liked *Kingdom Hearts*?

Was it possible to be halfway in love with someone based on that alone?

Before Jay could come up with a response that didn't make him look like a total nerd, Isla turned the tablet to Jay. "Your first appointment today is lunch with your sister and Min-ho Jong from the Corporate Flowers line at noon in her condo."

Jay checked his smartwatch. It was nearly eleven now. "Which sister?"

"Teresa."

Jay hugged his coffee close, stroking the edge lightly. "So lunch is at one. We have plenty of time. What should we do until then?"

Probably would be inappropriate to start a new game of *Kingdom Hearts III* with her, huh?

Isla blinked. "No, I said noon. That's what the calendar—"

Right. Isla hadn't learned about Teresa's allergy to punctuality or any of his family's other quirks yet.

She'd learn. She'd see how unglamorous everyone was underneath the glitzy clothes and contoured makeup. Everyone including himself.

She'd probably find out about his more unusual interests and judge him. His one particular interest in the bedroom was a deep-seated secret. Only Jay's romantic exes knew about it. The day Jay fired Caleb, he was greatly relieved he hadn't shared his kinks with Caleb.

Jay sighed, pushing away his memories of Caleb. "Teresa is chronically late. It'll be a waste of time to go there before one. Min-ho knows this too."

"Ah." Isla tapped the screen. "If you're sure you don't have to go until one, I'll let you get ready in peace. Is there anything you need?"

Jay scratched the back of his head. "What's after lunch?"

"A meeting with your mother at four, dinner at Iginla's with your stepfather at seven, and drinks with Stephen Polinsky at Cowboy Dreams around ten."

Cowboy Dreams. The worst place that serves overpriced moonshine along the East Coast. The nightmare multiplied when paired with someone like a hotel heir who loved being in the limelight.

Stephen was a tolerable friend until he got drunk. Then he'd start doing the weirdest shit. Stuff like shadowboxing on the dance floor and claiming he was gonna fight his sister's ex-husband, a rather famous comedian named Rian Goodwin. Not because Rian had actually done anything to Adaline Polinsky. Stephen just wanted to fight.

Jay would need his fade touched up if he was going to be photographed drinking in a dark corner and ignoring the dance floor.

"Set up an appointment at the salon for five." Jay pinched the bridge of his nose. "Other than that, I don't need anything."

"Understood!"

Isla busied herself with the tablet. Jay brought his coffee to his lips, though he was more fascinated with his assistant. What was Isla going to do until one?

He analyzed her outfit. Isla had a professional concept, but nothing stood out from the loose black dress pants and the white blouse. No accessories. Nothing that highlighted her assets, like her long legs and thick thighs.

He cleared his throat. Maybe a bit too loudly. "Want to go shopping for Milan before lunch?"

Isla looked up. "Shopping? For you? What should I buy?"

"No." Jay wandered over to the living room's massive window. He pretended to be interested in the view of the Manhattan skyline. "I thought you might, uh, want some new outfits for Milan."

"Oh."

The pep in Isla's voice died and fractured a part of Jay. His gaze snapped to her. Had he offended her?

Isla turned away from Jay. She fidgeted with the bag around her torso. He couldn't read her at all.

"Sorry," Jay mumbled. "I thought the prospect of clothes shopping would—"

"I don't have any money right now," Isla interrupted. "And I wouldn't want to use your credit card for my personal expenses."

Money?

That was an easily solved problem.

WHEN JAYDEN-JAMES HAD CLAIMED TO HAVE A solution to Isla's money woes, she thought he meant an advance on her paycheck. She did not expect a trip to the wardrobe floor.

A dozen rooms lined the hallway, each one filled with hundreds of garments. A different Hancock-Strauss line labeled each door.

Jayden-James stopped in front of a door with the word *Positive* painted on it.

"I don't have to borrow clothes from your company's stock." Isla peered inside the room. The mannequins in this world had different shapes than the others on this floor. The sight of plump mannequins stole Isla's breath.

"You're not borrowing. I'm gifting them to you." Jayden-James waltzed into the room. "Let me pick out some clothes for you, okay?"

Isla couldn't argue with the prospect of free clothes, nor could she resist the chance to be dressed by such a stylish man. The fashion icon had changed into a gray sweater and slipped on some purple jeans with black suspenders. The combination made no sense to Isla, but he looked fantastic.

"These are prototypes we never rolled out." Jayden-James entered the labyrinth of shirts, pants, and dresses. "Still good clothes."

"Do you often give clothes to people?" Isla followed him around the room. A colorful jungle of silks, furs, satin, velvet, wool, and cotton surrounded the pair. It was like being inside a thrift store, except quieter and without any underpaid employees.

"Uh-huh."

Something about Jayden-James had changed. Where he usually appeared withdrawn and uncertain, he now blazed with a sharp focus. His eyes had narrowed, his jaw had tightened, and he marched faster than Isla could keep up without tripping over her uncomfortable high heels.

Her boss was really, really hot.

Isla shook away the indecorous thoughts, choosing to distract herself with a silver chiffon dress. The bodice was lined with crystals, and it had a stretchy middle. She loved the stretchy middle.

Jayden-James turned to her. "You like that style?"

"Aren't you choosing my clothes for me?" Isla asked.

"The key to looking fashionable is to actually like what you're wearing." Jayden-James tucked a thumb under his suspender. "Confidence goes a long way. My sister, Samina, gets away with sweatpants in public because she loves them."

"I thought it was because she spends seventy dollars on them."

Jayden-James stared at Isla for far too many moments in silence. Panic shot through Isla's chest.

I shouldn't have said that. He's probably going to fire me.

"You might be right." Jayden-James wandered over to a different rack with dresses. "I take it you don't spend seventy dollars on sweatpants?"

A nervous belt of laughter escaped Isla. "Sweatpants should never cost more than ten dollars."

Jayden-James held a teal chiffon dress up to Isla. "I have to be honest. I don't remember the last time I spent only ten dollars."

"Yesterday." Isla blinked. "And today. That's a pretty color."

"Teals usually work great with red-heads who have your particular complexion." Jayden-James set the dress on an empty rack in the middle of the room and maneuvered to the next area. "What did I buy that costs so little?"

Isla inhaled sharply. She wanted to laugh. Or cry.

Hard to tell. "How much do you think coffee is, Mr. Hancock?"

"Oh."

Jayden-James pulled some shirts off the rack next to him and hung them with the teal dress. Isla assumed these were clothes he wanted her to try. Did Jayden-James have any idea how much the clothes his family sold cost?

Isla didn't either, really, but she knew any clothing line that had its own seasonal magazine was out of her budget.

"Um, can you not call me Mr. Hancock?" Jayden-James worked his jaw. "It's so formal."

"Agh!" Isla brought her hand to her mouth. "I'm sorry, uh, Jayden-James."

"Jay." He held up a paisley skirt. "Jay's fine."

"Yes, sir, Jay." Isla took the skirt from him. "Er, you do know my body is a little different, right? I might not look good in everything you select."

Jay tilted his head to the side. "In what way?"

Isla bunched the material in her fists. Heat crashed into her. The same humiliating heat every time she had to bring up being trans to someone who wasn't her roommates or mother.

He looked at her blankly. "Are you worried about your figure? You have a wonderful figure."

"I—" Wait. What did that mean? Another fire

started in Isla, this one confusingly pleased. "Uh, you know I'm trans, right? You saw my SuddenPic profile. It's right there."

Jay pressed his lips together. "That's right. Sorry. I forgot. I was more focused on other parts of your profile."

Other parts?

The fire raged on inside Isla, but now it crackled with a stinging sensation born from helplessness and indignation. She knew the discussion of her vocal activism would have to come up at some point, just like they would have to talk about her gender.

Noreen had been condescending earlier when she brought up student loans. Isla could only imagine Jay's position on the matter.

Jay's silence unnerved Isla as she mentally prepared for the inevitable fight. He continued to browse clothes, adding more tops and pants to the center rack.

Isla's throat tightened as she addressed Jay. "Do you have questions about my involvement with the EFSLRA?"

"Huh?" Jay stopped in his tracks. "The what?"

"The Ex-Students For Student Loan Reformation Alliance."

Jay held a beige wool jacket close to him. His puzzled expression plunged Isla into equal confusion.

"You said you were focused on other parts of my SuddenPic profile." Isla fanned herself. "Didn't you mean my activism?"

"Are those the people you're with in most of your pictures?" Jay asked. "With the signs?"

Pictures. Did he only look at her pictures?

"Yes." Isla clenched her fists and folded her arms across her chest. "I would never get to browse such fancy clothes with my pitiful socioeconomic background as it is. My student loan debt has kept me jailed for years from affluent adventures."

Jay leaned against the rack. "You need your loans paid off? I could take care of that if it'll help you."

Isla sucked in her breath and willed herself not to say anything she would regret. He almost sounded sincere. There was no way he could be that nice.

"It's not just me with debt, sir, Jay."

Jay picked some lint off the coat. "Jay, okay? I'm not a knight."

"Sorry." Isla took the coat from Jay. "Should I add this to the rack?"

"No, it looks terrible now that I see you with it." Jay grabbed it from her. "What's the issue with the student loans?"

Where to begin? "I'm working hard with other people to ensure the country makes education more accessible and helps people who are struggling financially because of their student loans."

"Is it really that big of an issue?"

A chuckle forced its way out of Isla, an effort to keep the subject light and her heart protected. "If anyone ever feels lonely, they should try missing a student loan payment."

Jay didn't laugh at her joke.

In fact, Jay gazed at her in such a way that made Isla want to lower her guard. Perhaps he was *so* rich, he truly had no idea what Americans were suffering. Hell, he didn't know a butterscotch cappuccino with two shots of espresso was six dollars.

Would it be bad to trust him with a part of her heart?

"It's bad." Isla's voice grew hard, serious. "The fact I have a job working for you is such a blessing. I'm grateful you have given me a chance to get out of debt. I hope the rallies and stuff I attend don't bother you. I can't give up on it, not while so many are hurting."

As soon as her last sentence escaped her, Isla feared she had crossed a line with her new boss.

That fear was quickly erased by the gentleness in Jay's voice. "You don't have to give up anything for me. As long as you're not promoting hate toward a marginalized group or selling pictures of my sisters to the tabloids, like my old assistant."

"They did what?!" Isla gasped. "Oh, Jay, I'm so sorry. I would never."

Jay's gloomy expression nearly broke her heart. "I hope so."

She'd prove her reliability to Jay. Prove he had been right in picking a new assistant.

THREE

THE CONFERENCE IN MILAN PROVED TERRIFICALLY boring for Jay.

He couldn't add meaningful discussion to the upcoming fashion show or flip through applications for models. He was there to shadow his mother as she led everything. Hold sensitive documents for her and ensure she finished eating meals instead of getting lost in work. Look good in paparazzi photos of the Hancock-Strauss family. Wonder when he would become something more than a professional son.

At least it was a nice break from all the partying with Stephen he had done over the last two weeks. Poor Isla had to drive Jay home at three AM a few times.

What else was Jay supposed to do as a

professional son, though, when his mom didn't need some family arm candy?

Would he ever get to hold a real position in the company? Would he ever get to have a family dinner where he was celebrated for his successes?

The subject of a new fashion line for college students came up during a meeting, pulling Jay from his cloud of self-doubts.

"Are they going to be able to afford our clothes?" Jay whispered to his mother while the proposer continued his PowerPoint show.

Dee stared at him over the rim of her violet sunglasses. Even in a dark room, she never took them off.

"I think most college students are broke." Jay pulled up Isla's SuddenPic on his phone. "Isla does some kind of activism about student loans."

"Student loans don't keep people from buying clothes." Dee glanced at the phone. "I suggest you do your own research. Now let's pay attention to the proposal."

Jay watched the PowerPoint presentation for another few minutes. His mother's comment never quite left him, though, so he took his phone back out.

Perhaps he could just pay off everyone's student loan debts. What good was wealth if he didn't spend it? How much debt could Americans possibly be in from education?

Search results told him $1.5 trillion.

All right. That idea was tabled.

Following his mother's advice—while ignoring her occasional glares—Jay continued reading more into the student loan crisis.

Tuition Continues to Skyrocket, Leaves Students Without Options

Interest Rates for Borrower to Increase

U.S. Economy in Trouble, Thanks to Student Loans

With each article Jay read, the more astonished he became at how utterly fucked up the system was.

It shouldn't have surprised him, considering how much the government loved to siphon life out of anyone. Still, he understood why Isla had resolved to make things better for people—why she had glowed with determination when she told him she wouldn't give up her activism.

Admiration for Isla bloomed in Jay's chest. If he could be a little more like her, he could be something besides a professional son.

All the articles, numbers, and stories about student loans clouded Jay's thoughts, long after the meeting ended.

Reporters waited outside of the hotel as Jay

journeyed with his mother for lunch. Noreen and Isla escorted them.

Dee began answering questions in Italian. She often gave the reporters exactly four minutes of her time before pointing them to Noreen.

Jay spoke Italian, too, but reporters rarely bothered him when his mother was around. She attracted people like the Trevi Fountain; he was the place nearby that served gelato. One can get gelato anywhere. There was only one Dee Hancock-Strauss.

Jay glanced at Isla. Her eyes were as wide as dinner plates as she took in the circus of flashing lights and microphones. She looked amazing in a loose-knit sweater, plaid skirt, and black leggings. He rarely got the chance to dress people, and it pleased him to see one of his outfits on someone besides himself.

Her pale cheeks left him worried, though.

"Are you okay?" he asked Isla. "Too many people?"

"Huh?" Isla gripped the violet lanyard around her neck. "I'm fine! Is there something I can get for you?"

Jay shook his head.

"Jayden-James!" A reporter waved to him. "Can I get a moment?"

Huh. An English-speaking person. Not unusual, but they still preferred to talk to his mother.

"Hello," Jay said, for lack of any better way to

start an impromptu interview. Isla distanced herself almost immediately.

The reporter held the mic out to Jay. "We understand a university line has been proposed. What does it mean to dress the part for academic success?"

Jay supposed he should have said something about how college students shouldn't wear pajamas to class, but the articles he had read weighed heavily on his mind. "Do you know about the student loan debt crisis?"

The reporter blinked.

In Jay's peripheral vision, Isla mirrored the same surprise.

"It's good if college students are well-dressed, I suppose." Jay brought a thumb to his lapel, focusing on the crystal brooch accentuating his purple blazer. "But is fashion accessible to them when they have to take out massive loans to pay for education?"

The reporter continued holding their mic to Jay. More photographers turned to him.

Jay's gaze swiveled to Isla. "Sorry if that's a weird response, but we can't design a fashion line aimed at college students while ignoring their problems. We are doing extensive research."

A gorgeous smile slowly unraveled across Isla's face.

Research.

Was that all he could do, or could he do more?

ISLA REFRAINED FROM READING THE COMMENTS TO online articles, but she found herself constantly refreshing the article a popular gossip site had posted about Jay's earlier remarks. Even while she got ready in her hotel room for dinner, she couldn't keep her eyes off the tablet.

Some people remarked on his outfit or talked about how handsome he was (one particularly inspired poster referred to Jay as "Dapper Daddy" and invited him to "raw" them). Others complained about the high cost of Hancock-Strauss clothes. Most discussed student loans.

People shouldn't take out student loans if they can't repay them.

My $80,000 debt is finally paid off after fifteen years! I don't want anyone else to go through that.

The job market doesn't favor marginalized people, especially people of color. How are we supposed to pay off our loans?

It's not fair to make debt repayment easier or erase debts if other people worked hard to pay their loans off!

In the years Isla had spent with the EFSLRA, she

understood there was no perfect solution to the problem that would please everyone. She also knew nothing would get done if people didn't rally for change.

Having a celebrity like Jay mention the crisis helped. He probably wouldn't talk about it again, but he had done more than most rich people had.

Isla studied the pictures included with the article.

Not a single photo showed off Jay's stunning eyes. For someone who made a lot of eye contact in person, the kind that makes one dizzy with anticipation, he never met a camera head on.

Isla's phone buzzed, pulling her away from the tablet.

Come get me when you're ready, Jay said.

It was preposterous to have dinner in Milan with her celebrity boss, but Jay had insisted on it. Something to celebrate Isla's first time in Europe.

Isla smoothed the fabric of the teal dress along her middle.

This was the only time she'd let Jay treat her to such an extravagant meal. In the future, after she caught up on some past-due bills, she would buy him an equally nice dinner. Something to thank him for showing her college hadn't been a waste.

Isla ambled down the hall. The family owned this floor of the hotel since they flew in to Milan often.

Rather than numbers, each door had its resident's name on it.

She knocked on Jay's door. He answered it almost immediately and nearly caused Isla to faint from his splendidness.

Jayden-James Hancock epitomized the very definition of divine. The gold tones of his floral tuxedo jacket made his smooth, brown skin glow. Teal butterflies were embroidered among the flowers, the same teal as her dress. His eyeliner was thicker than usual with a few blue sparkles along the edges. No glasses.

The most glittery thing about Jay tonight, though, was his smile.

She hadn't seen his lips curve upward before. His smile could easily turn a billion dollars into worthless scraps of paper.

A wisp of heat crept into her cheeks. Isla suddenly understood that online commenter begging Jay to raw them.

Jay's smile only lasted for a moment. When he went back to his usual, uncomfortable self, disappointment washed through Isla.

Isla adjusted the shoulder strap of her bag. "You look fantastic."

Despite all the new stuff she had, she hadn't managed to let go of this vital accessory. Every button on her bag told a story—her favorite anime, every indie rock band she had seen live, her college extracurriculars, words she found comforting (*sunshine, cats, tomorrow*). The bag let the world know more about Isla Dyer at a glance than her SuddenPic profile ever could.

She expected Jay to comment on the bag. Remark that it didn't vibe with the opulence associated with her job.

Instead, sincerity shined in his voice as he said, "I was thinking the same of you."

God, what a shame he was her boss and not...something else...

Isla forced out a chuckle. "The cab is ready downstairs."

"Great."

They walked to the elevator together, at a pace slow enough Isla wouldn't trip over her heels.

Isla pressed the button. "Thanks for bringing up the student loan debt crisis earlier. You didn't have to."

"It was relevant to the conversation." Jay gestured for Isla to enter the open elevator first. "My SuddenPic mentions are a disaster now though."

"What do you think of their comments?" Isla selected the first floor. "Or what you read, anyway. I assume you didn't read much."

Jay leaned against the wall next to Isla. "No, I read everything they said. It's a serious, worldwide problem. Some of my followers were telling me about their issues. Even in countries with free tuition, students have to borrow for expenses."

Isla gaped at him.

Was it bad that she was more attracted to him now?

She silently chastised herself. She shouldn't be interested in men just because they showed a basic level of decency toward other humans.

"Can I boost the EFSLRA on my SuddenPic?" Jay glanced at her. "Does it need donations? I don't really understand how it works."

This man was making it really, really hard to be disinterested in him.

Her thoughts drifted to her first day of work. The stunning, powerful Noreen inside her messy, cramped apartment.

Isla took a deep breath. "That's so sweet of you. You don't have to involve yourself. I know it's not an issue that concerns you—"

Jay met her eyes. "It concerns me."

They reached the first floor of the hotel, but Jay didn't make an effort to leave the elevator. Isla remained in the box with him, captivated by his serious gaze.

"I've never done a day's hard work in my life," Jay said as the doors closed. Vulnerability shined in his voice. "You work hard all the time. Most people do. The difference between us is money."

Was he truly baring his heart to her?

Jay adjusted his cuff. "I can't pay off everyone's debts, but surely I can do something with my money and fame."

"You can." Isla pressed the open button and tried to ignore the giddiness brewing in her chest. "You must be hungry. We should hurry."

She started to leave, but Jay grabbed her hand.

They hadn't made any kind of physical contact before. It frustrated Isla how much she enjoyed having his warm grip around her fingers while his eyes blazed with that confident determination he only bore around a room full of clothes.

"Can we take a raincheck?" Jay asked. "I want to start helping right away."

Isla made no effort to break away from him. "Are you sure? Aren't you hungry? You always dine around seven, and it's almost ten."

"We can order room service." Jay squeezed her hand. "Please let me finally be useful."

Her heart flipped.

Isla didn't care at all for five course dinners. She cared about ensuring people could get an education and still be able to eat something besides instant noodles.

She also understood how frustrating it was to feel useless. Unqualified.

If her boss shared the same values, she wanted to work alongside him.

FOUR

ONCE THE CONFERENCE IN MILAN ENDED, JAY AND
his mother were the only members of their family to
fly back home immediately. The long flight to New
York was nothing new to Jay, but the snoozing Isla
next to him a pleasant addition.

She had been so excited going to Milan—
admiring the sleeper beds, large screens, and every
other luxury that came with first class—that she
didn't dare blink in fear of missing a moment. It had
been precious to watch her then, but Jay found
himself more enamored by Isla's present condition.
She had worked so hard all week in Milan with
helping Jay build his awareness campaign on top of
her regular assistant duties. To finally see her replace
her tablet with a worn paperback Alyssa Cole novel
and catch some z's...

Jay swallowed hard.

His smartwatch lit up with a message from his mother. *Come see me.*

Leave it to Signora Strauss to text her son a few seats away instead of getting up herself. Jay supposed they would go over a magazine layout or a new sketch. Nothing that actually required his opinion; it was just how Dee bonded with her children.

As Jay got up, he pulled his blanket out of the sleeper's drawer. He set Isla's book aside and covered her with the blanket. Before he walked away, he tucked a few locks of Isla's silky curls behind her ear.

It was nice to take care of his assistant for once. For the past two weeks, Isla greeted him with coffee and a smile every morning, and she made sure he was ten minutes early to every appointment. Hiring her had been a fabulous decision.

His gaze meandered to her soft-looking lips. It would have been nice if he had been gutsy enough to ask her on a date like he initially wanted, but he just wasn't meant to be with her in that way. Even his attempt at a romantic-but-still-professional dinner had gone up in smoke because his insecure self wanted to do some good.

Jay sighed. Some drafted social media posts would go live in a few hours. His campaign would begin soon, one he had no idea how his fans would react.

Did an heir to a multi-billion dollar company have a place championing for more transparency in the loan process and better loan rates?

Another message came through on his watch. He didn't need to read it to know it was his mother.

He reluctantly left Isla's side and joined his mother in her suite. She practically had a room to herself on flights. Her corner sleeper was guarded with a privacy curtain, stocked with endless bottles of sparkling water, and had a couch for her to run meetings.

Dee patted the empty spot on the vinyl sofa next to her without looking up from her tablet.

Jay kissed her on the forehead before sitting down. "What's going on, Ma?"

"I thought you might want to explain this to me." Dee handed her tablet to Jay.

Jay didn't need more than a split second to realize what he was looking at—his SuddenPic post that wasn't supposed to be up yet.

Oh. Shit. He might have set the posts to go live at midnight in Milan, not New York City.

He bit his lip. Isla wouldn't have made such a blunder.

"I checked the cloud, and there is an interview with *Mornings with Ross Steel* scheduled for Tuesday." Dee stared at him over the rim of her sunglasses.

"You never do live interviews. Do you plan on talking about student loans there too? Don't you think you should have consulted me or Noreen before starting such a stunt?"

Jay set the tablet down between them. Apprehension tightened his chest. "It's not a stunt, Ma. It's an effort to be useful."

"Useful?" Dee adjusted her yellow beaded scarf. "In what way?"

The tightness in Jay's chest increased, causing his mouth to remain closed as he concentrated on breathing. As close as he was to his mother, he had never been able to share any of his insecurities with her.

Why should he? There wasn't a problem that money couldn't solve in the Hancock-Strauss family. Even when Caleb snapped those indecent photos of Samina, the family had been able to buy the photos back from the tabloids and pay Caleb enough to disappear from the East Coast.

That bastard had made a fortune being deceitful. Good, honest people like Isla struggled to put bread on the dinner table.

Jay would use his money to solve the student loan debt crisis, somehow. There was more to him than being a prop for his family's feel-good stories.

"Why student loans?" Dee picked her tablet up.

"Are you trying to tell me you want to head the college student line with your expertise?"

...

Huh?

"Run your campaign," Dee said. "Do your research. Get to know our potential market better. If you prove successful, I'll give you the fashion line."

Jay certainly hadn't approached his new journey with the goal of getting a fashion line. In fact, he hadn't anticipated his mother to notice at all. As long as her children weren't committing crimes against humanity, Dee left the family image to Noreen.

Jay's heart jumped to his throat. For his mother to finally offer him a role as something more than a professional son...

He couldn't say no.

Getting up at four AM for a nine AM interview wasn't Isla's idea of an excellent time, but the set of *Mornings with Ross Steel* proved worthwhile. All during Milan, she had to watch Jay disappear behind a closed door for hours at a time. She never had any idea if he needed anything during those long meetings.

Here, she got to help Jay get ready. While the

stylist prepared his makeup and hair, Isla went over Jay's outfit (a long-sleeved white fishnet top and the world's skinniest black denim jeans) with a lint roller and spritzed it with water to smooth some wrinkles.

"You don't have to go through so much trouble," Jay said, watching her from the mirror in his chair.

Isla waved to him. "It's no trouble. Are you okay? Live television must be scary."

"It's okay," he answered. "No different than when someone stops me on the street."

"But you always—"

Their conversation was interrupted by the stylist announcing she had finished. Jay thanked the stylist as she packed up her supplies. Isla, too, began to leave the dressing room so Jay could have his privacy while he changed.

"Hold on." Jay undid the top button of his shirt. "What were you going to say? I always what?"

Isla waited for the stylist to leave before she finished her sentence. This gave her time to reconsider her words. It was probably going to be rude to tell her boss he always looked like he was two steps away from a panic attack in public, even though it was the truth.

The increasing warmth in the small dressing room caused sweat to run down the back of Isla's neck. "Can I give you some advice?"

Jay nodded.

Okay. Here went nothing. She could be honest and gentle, just like him.

"You always look nervous around cameras." Isla twirled a strand of hair around her finger. "There's not a single picture of you on the internet where your pretty eyes can be enjoyed in their full glory."

Agh! Too honest!

She debated leaving right then and hiding in the closest bathroom, but a ghost of a smile teased Jay's mouth. That little quirk held Isla in place.

He gestured for her to continue. A quiet, tender curiosity emanated from Jay. How could he be so reassuring without uttering a single word?

Isla exhaled slowly. "You have a magnetic quality about you when you're putting together outfits or talking about the student loan debt crisis with me. If you could channel that same energy when you're doing an interview and look directly at the camera, people will watch more intently."

Jay undid his second button. "Do you think people really want to watch me?"

A lump developed in Isla's throat as Jay's bare collarbone became exposed.

"People have never been seriously interested in me before." Jay brought his hand to the third button. "It's always seemed pointless to face a camera."

"Really?" Isla gripped her bag, willing herself not to look if he continued undressing. "You're the most interesting person I know."

Jay's lips twitched again.

She wished he would bless her with another dazzler. All Isla wanted at that moment was to see him smile.

The large, red LED clock in the dressing room snapped to 8:35. Jay had to be on standby in fifteen minutes.

"You should get changed," Isla said. "Don't worry about what I told you if it makes you uncomfortable."

Before another word could be exchanged between them, Isla dipped out of the room.

At exactly nine on the dot, Ross Steel's show returned from a commercial break. Isla stood to the side, right in the line of view where Jay would be sitting. She had notes prepared on her tablet to show Jay in case he forgot an important statistic or the source of a study.

Ross's loud, slightly grating voice rolled through the room.

"For the first time ever, I'm pleased to announce I have a male member of the Hancock-Strauss family with us!" The middle-aged host clapped his hands. "His sisters have graced our presence, and now we finally get to chat with Jayden-James Hancock! Let's welcome him to *our* family."

The audience burst into cheers as Jay shuffled onto the set. He waved to the crowd briefly and shook hands with Ross. The pair chatted for a few minutes about Jay's sisters before the topic slowly shifted to Milan.

Isla unlocked the tablet, ready to put it to use. A wave of nerves hit her as soon as she saw the EFSLRA in her notes. She had been so concerned with Jay, she had nearly forgotten what he came here to do.

It was surreal to have the little-known organization she was involved with escalating to new heights. They had received a tremendous financial boost, thanks to Jay's platform.

"Jayden-James, you started showing a keen interest in student loans." Ross shuffled his notecards while some of the crowd cheered. "There have been numerous articles about the statements you've made. Are you, perhaps, struggling to pay off your student loans?"

A laugh colored the end of Ross's question, but his joke wasn't met with any hint of amusement on Jay's end. Jay fiddled with his Rolex as his unsure gaze slowly turned to Isla.

Isla flashed him the biggest smile she could

muster, willing all of her good energies to magically sneak into Jay's body.

Jay suddenly sat up straight in his chair. His attention had shifted to Ross. A spark of the fire Isla adored flickered in her boss's visage.

"I don't have to struggle with loans to empathize with other people." The softness always present in Jay's voice had disappeared. His new, hardened tone nearly caused Isla to drop her tablet. "The root of this problem is a severe lack of empathy from people in power."

The audience went wild with Jay's comment. While their agreement thundered through the studio, Isla caught a glimpse of the monitor above her. The screen had captured Jay staring directly at the camera with that determination she had first witnessed on the wardrobe floor.

A strange mix of pride and sorrow rang through Isla. Part of her had enjoyed knowing such a private side to Jay. Now the whole world would know just how intense and sexy he could be.

Isla's phone buzzed multiple times in her pocket. She checked it immediately—her screen was filled with push notifications every time Jay's name was used on SuddenPic. People were talking about him; they were talking about student loans.

All the softness Jay had temporarily pushed aside

fluttered through Isla as she continued watching the interview. Jay was so amazing. He had been perceptive enough to assess Isla would be a good assistant after only one conversation, a quality she still couldn't see in herself. He had given her an incredibly well-paying job that used all the skills she learned while studying communications. Jay treated the first cup of cappuccino of the day like it was his best friend, called his mother every day to ask if she had eaten lunch, and played cute video games any time he had an opening in his schedule.

His softness bloomed in Isla's chest, made a home in her heart.

FIVE

The months following the interview on *Mornings with Ross Steel* opened more doors than Jay ever knew existed. People asked him to write blog posts, he did interviews on every news and entertainment channel in the States, universities in Canada and Europe invited him to give lectures, he attended rallies in D.C., and he partnered with the EFSLRA for a fundraiser. Any chance he got to talk, he seized it—even going on Rian Goodwin's show.

His blustering schedule left no room for brunches with his sisters, clubbing with heirs, or shadowing his mother. Fortunately, he had Isla to field his calls and ensure he never missed one of his new commitments.

As much as he had worked during the last few months, she had worked three times as hard. All with a smile on her face. She never complained, not once.

As soon as he got the fashion line, as soon as he proved he was something more than a professional son, he'd be sure to give Isla a proper gift to thank her. The buttons on her messenger bag suggested she liked *Cardcaptor Sakura*. Maybe they could take a trip to Japan and buy all the merchandise she'd ever want? Or perhaps she'd be more satisfied with a new apartment, filled to the brim with romance books?

A message from Isla waited on Jay's phone when he stepped out of the shower. He had plans to meet his mother and stepfather for dinner so they could talk about tomorrow's photo shoot. It wasn't every day Jay would be the sole family member on a magazine cover.

Your parents won't be coming back from Montreal until early tomorrow morning. There's a bad thunderstorm keeping their plane grounded.

A sweet, delightful high shot through Jay. Nothing was better than cancelled plans. *Does this mean my evening is free?*

Yes, Isla replied. *Do you want me to book a reservation somewhere for you or have the cook prepare you a meal?*

Jay rubbed his jaw as he stared at his phone. He had a free evening. Isla possibly had a free evening now too.

Is there anything you want to do? Jay asked. *You*

probably haven't had time to see your roommates or family in a while.

Hardly more than a couple of seconds passed before Isla answered. *It's Saturday—my roommates are working. Mom lives in Rhode Island.*

A smile sprung to Jay's face. Isla was free. They could do something together without any pressure to get from point A to point B.

Want to bring some tacos over? Jay asked. *You haven't gotten to play KH3 yet. Tonight could be a great time to start.*

Really!?!?!?

All the heart emojis following Isla's text sent Jay floating into space.

Jay opted to change into a plain T-shirt and sweatpants. He figured there wasn't any point in getting glamorous for an evening on his couch, especially when this wasn't a date.

A small evening like this could never be a date. Dates were romantic dinners in Milan with stars glittering in the sky and champagne bubbling in glasses. Big, splashy gestures of affection.

Isla must have been on the same wavelength as him. She showed up in black leggings and the pink parka she had worn the day they met.

"Should we eat first?" Isla pointed to the big bag

of Tex-Mex goodness. "I don't want to make a mess on your nice furniture."

"We have a lot of cutscenes in the opening." Jay swiped the bag from her and set it on the table in front of the television. "There's beer and soda in the fridge. What do you want?"

"I can get it," Isla protested. "I'm your assistant."

"Tonight, you are my guest." Jay wandered to the kitchen. "Relax."

"Uh, okay. Beer, please."

His appetite momentarily dissipated when he returned to the living room with a couple of beers. Isla had unpacked the food and spread the array of soft shell tacos along the table neatly, with plenty of sauces and napkins accompanying their meal. Isla had removed her parka, revealing a blue tank top that exposed a generous amount of cleavage. Her long, vibrant curls spilled over her shoulders as she waited for him on the couch, gazing at him with those soft brown eyes he adored.

She looked marvelously comfortable.

"Do you want anything else before we start playing?" Jay asked after they ate for a couple of minutes. "Ice cream? A masseuse? We can get it delivered."

Isla smiled. "This is more than enough."

"We've worked our asses off lately." Jay turned on the console. "We deserve a break. Both of us."

"It's okay for me to work hard. You're paying me so much money." She shook her head. "I really appreciate you giving me this dream job. I still can't believe you took one look at me and decided I would be a good assistant."

A sliver of guilt crept up Jay's spine.

"The money has helped out tremendously. I think I can even start going back to therapy." Isla paused. "Well, whenever I have a day off, I guess."

The guilt wrapped itself around Jay's neck and threatened to choke him. He set his food down. "Just schedule your appointments and take time off as needed. You don't have to be with me for every second."

"But that's my job!" Doubt darkened Isla's bright face. "It's not like the therapy is ultra important to my mental health. As long as I can afford my hormones and antidepressants, I'm mostly fine. Therapy just balances out my confusing gender thoughts. Like, do I always have to wear lipstick and high heels to prove I'm a woman?"

"Sounds important to me." Jay leaned against the couch, opening a beer with his platinum bottle opener. "Gender is confusing. I never understood why I have to justify my love for clothes and makeup. Why can't we be allowed to wear what we want?"

"Exactly." Isla sighed and leaned against the couch as well. "I miss a lot of clothes I used to wear before I came out as trans, but I'm afraid people will ask why I bothered transitioning."

Jay handed the beer to Isla. Their arms brushed each other as he did so, sparking the neurons in his brain with possibilities. Possibilities he quickly threw out the window.

While he missed Isla's sweet, bubbly smile, he appreciated being able to witness this side of her. Reading her public SuddenPic updates with gender musings was one thing; hearing her worries in person felt more personal.

"You should be allowed to parade in suits or whatever society thinks is masculine all you want." Jay opened the other beer for himself. "Just like I should be allowed to don some lovely lingerie around my bed partner without being judged."

Instantly, Jay wished he could undo the last minute of his life. Why had he revealed such a personal secret so easily?

Isla held her drink to her lips. "Lingerie?"

Jay met Isla's gaze. The only thing keeping him from combusting into an overheated ball of awkwardness was the cold beer in his hand.

The longer Jay stared at Isla, though, the more he realized Isla would never sell him out to a tabloid magazine or mock him. She had accepted his tattooed eyeliner, plethora of moisturizers, and inability to buy his own coffee with a gentle grace.

He trusted her.

"Yeah, lingerie." To Jay's surprise, his lips curved upward as he spoke. "I look damn good in lace and ribbons."

The joy he was used to seeing on Isla returned. Her cheeks glowed a gorgeous shade of pink. "I bet you do."

Jay laughed. "You don't think it's weird?"

"The exact opposite." Isla patted his shoulder. Her hand rested on him while she continued talking, a gesture he didn't mind at all. "You keep being you."

Jay couldn't wipe the grin off his face. "Thanks. I appreciate it."

"And thank you for letting me vent about my feelings." Isla's hand slid down his arm. She smiled at him so genuinely, sparking more ideas in Jay's brain. "I promise I'll make an appointment for therapy soon."

"Good." Jay leaned forward and started the game. Their knees bumped into each other, but neither of them made an effort to create distance between them.

Jay relished how close they were. How electric every little touch was.

When *Kingdom Heart III*'s opening notes filled the room and Isla's eyes widened with delight, Jay realized he had been wrong about romance.

He had taken his past significant others to plenty of expensive dinners in Milan, but tonight—surrounded by tacos, pajamas, video games, light touches, and shared secrets—was the most romantic date Jay had ever experienced.

Too bad Isla would never view it as such.

JAY HAD AN ARMY OF STYLISTS FOR HIS PHOTO shoot with *Business Idols*, leaving Isla with little to do except think about last night. Hanging out at Jay's had been magical, a great respite from the rollercoaster ride of the past months. Still, Isla preferred to work.

Work made it easier to push down the racing heartbeat she got every time she greeted Jay in the mornings. Work buried the lust Isla experienced when Jay wore suspenders or ranted about the lack of loan forgiveness options for veterinarians. Work gave her a sense of purpose.

Thanks to Jay, Isla had a job that she was good at.

His compliments filled her in ways romance novels and cappuccinos could not. She loved working for a boss who was passionate about student loans *and* approached everyone with gentle empathy.

Together, they were changing the world, a little bit at a time.

On a quieter level, Isla finally believed she was qualified to be an assistant.

A stern voice pulled Isla back to reality. "Hard to believe that's the same Jayden-James who used to hide behind my skirt at the sight of a camera."

Isla turned to her left. "Hello, Signora Strauss. I'm glad your flight finally arrived. Is Mr. Strauss here? Can I get you anything?"

No response came from Dee. She removed her violet sunglasses and quietly watched Jay sparkle in the center of the spotlights.

Isla couldn't blame Dee for being mesmerized. For this particular shoot, the photographers had Jay pose on an ornate throne while surrounded by piles of past due bills. Glitter dusted his twists, gold roses had been painted along the side of his face, and he gazed at the camera with a serious intensity.

Jay owned the set. If he wanted to own the world, he could.

Noreen approached Isla and Dee. She motioned for Isla to step aside.

"Yes?" Isla asked once they were alone. "Can I get something for you?"

"No." Noreen smirked. "Quite the opposite. I wanted to see if I could get something for you. This is all because of you, Isla."

Isla gulped. Was that a compliment or...?

Noreen gestured to the menagerie of cameras. "You did in three months what Signora Strauss has been trying to do for years."

"What is that?" Isla hooked her thumb around her lanyard. She still got intimidated around Noreen, even after all these months.

"Jayden-James is ready for more responsibility with the company." Noreen pulled out her phone. "It wouldn't have happened without you. What do you say to a bonus? Should I give it to you directly, or would you prefer the family make a sizable contribution to the EFSLRA as Jay's parting gift from the campaign?"

Parting gift?!

Isla swallowed hard. "What do you mean?"

Noreen smiled. "Just watch Jay's reaction when Dee talks to him. He's getting something he's been wanting."

Before Isla could press Noreen, the lead photographer called for a break.

Dee waltzed over to Jay, sunglasses back on her face. Jay's stylists allowed Dee to approach Jay first.

Isla often gave Jay his space when he spoke to someone, especially a member of his family, but she couldn't stay away from the conversation this time.

"Hey, Ma." Jay, still seated in the throne, flashed Isla a quick smile. "Did you have breakfast?"

"It's lunch time now." Dee craned her head to the side. "Why don't we eat together when you're done here and discuss how we'll announce the college student line with you as the lead creative director?"

Jay gaped at Dee.

The melodic rhythm of photographers changing lenses, technicians adjusting lights, and stylists preparing Jay's makeup fizzled to white noise as Isla focused on Dee.

"We'll also start retiring this campaign of yours." Dee pointed to the pile of bills. "You don't need to do anymore research on the market."

"Research?" Isla repeated aloud, unable to mask the shock. "What does that mean, Jay?"

Jay's ensuing silence hit Isla's stomach like a wrecking ball.

"One needs to do research to sell," Dee answered. "He has done an excellent job in this campaign to prove he's qualified to become a lead creative director."

Isla stared at Jay. Was all of Jay's activism just to get a fashion line?

Had she been wrong about him?

Jay jumped to his feet. "Wait! Ma, you're making this sound different than what it is. Isla, listen to me."

"You lied to me." Isla glared at him. "You made me think you were interested in helping people."

Jay took a step toward Isla. "Of course I want to help people. This campaign is genuine."

"It's possible to be both altruistic and maintain a keen sense of business," Noreen said. "A few months of dedicated community service is fabulous work."

Dee nodded.

Community service.

"And now Jay's done with his community service since he's getting his own fashion line?" Isla's throat burned with fury as she spoke. "Should I cancel the meeting with the lobbyists in Washington on Thursday?"

"No, Isla, please listen to me." Jay grabbed Isla's hand. "Yes, I wanted a fashion line, but I wanted to help people more."

Isla jerked away from him, maintaining her glare. She'd probably never, ever smile around him ever again.

Jay wheezed. "Please, let's go grab a coffee, and I'll explain properly. You know I'm not good with words on the fly. You know better than anyone how awkward I am. Even my attempt to ask you out was an abomination."

Huh?

Isla placed a hand on her chest. "What do you mean? Ask me out?"

Jay glanced at his mother and Noreen, then he shifted his gaze to the floor. He ran a finger along the length of his tie. "When we met. I invited you to Milan because I wanted to go on a date, but you, uh, you interpreted it as a job offer, and—"

No.

No, no, no.

Tears sprung to Isla's eyes. "You didn't mean to hire me?"

Jay's mouth flapped, but no words manifested.

His silence hit her again, but this time, the wrecking ball crashed into her entire body. Her whole reason for being here had been a lie. In the end, her degree was worthless. She wasn't qualified in the least to be an assistant. Jay probably kept her around as an act of charity.

Isla didn't need his sympathy.

Isla threw the lanyard with her ID badge on the ground. She shoved her beloved button-covered messenger bag with all the devices Noreen had given her back into the secretary's possession.

Noreen started to say something, but Dee held her hand up. Noreen's lips formed a thin line at once.

"I'll return the car fobs tomorrow." Isla wiped her eyes. "You don't have to worry about this community service anymore."

Jay slumped into the throne chair. His crestfallen visage almost seemed sincere. Once upon a time, Isla would have thought his hurt was real.

Isla left the glimmering king where he deserved to be, surrounded by props and people who only cared about money.

SIX

It had been eight hours since Isla quit, and Jay was already falling apart.

Jay stood inside the same Monahan's where he met Isla, trying to figure out what to order. He couldn't order a butterscotch cappuccino. It'd taste too much like happiness.

Why was coffee so hard?

A message lit up on Jay's smartwatch.

Where are you? His mother asked. *We've been waiting for an hour.*

Oh. Yeah. He was supposed to have dinner with his mother and stepfather.

Jay flicked some lingering glitter off Isla's messenger bag, missing her more than ever. Isla would have ensured he showed up fifteen minutes early.

As soon as Jay stepped outside and inhaled the cool spring air, he desperately wished he could rewind to yesterday. 24 hours ago, he had been enveloped in Isla's warmth, playing games and eating way too many tacos.

He had gone to bed last night with a smile on his face. Tonight, he would go to bed covered in depression-flavored ice cream.

Jay eventually reached the restaurant. To his surprise, his sisters were at the table as well. It had been a long time since the whole family had gathered for the same meal.

Teresa held a glass of wine up as soon as Jay sat down. "Let's have a toast."

"I agree." Samina rubbed Jay's shoulder. "Look at our little big brother, leading an entire fashion line."

"We're very proud of you," Jay's stepfather chimed in. "With all the work you've been putting in for research, we know the college student line will be a success."

"It wasn't research," Jay mumbled, fiddling with his watch. "I actually care about this cause."

"I know you do." Dee poured a glass of wine for Jay. "You're finally serious enough to run a business. It's been hard to give you responsibility when you were just playing all the time. This campaign has matured you."

Jay stared at his mother. What was he supposed to have been doing this whole time if he didn't have any responsibility to prove he was more than a professional son?

"Our family doesn't have to separate from the activism, of course." Dee held her glass up. "But for now, we should focus our efforts on your successful launch of the college fashion line."

"To Jayden-James!" Samina called loudly.

Teresa raised her voice. "To our new lead creative director!"

As everyone clinked their glasses, Jay realized this title wasn't worth what he lost. Isla had always seen him as something besides a professional son. She had treated him as a boss, an ally, a friend, a confidant.

He could find other things to do. Being a lead creative director without his tall, sweet, lovely goddess would be pointless.

While everyone downed their wine, Jay excused himself to the bathroom and called Noreen.

USUALLY, IT WASN'T A GOOD IDEA TO ANSWER THE door in the derelict apartment building when one wasn't expecting guests. That guideline became a hard rule after 10 PM.

Isla's roommates, however, never listened to rules.

Isla sat on the corner of the couch, pretending to watch whatever true crime documentary series Garrett was obsessed with while Dominick opened the door. Isla hadn't told them yet about her sudden unemployment. She couldn't bring herself to confess that she was a messenger bag-less failure with a useless degree.

Not to mention some part of her felt horrible for ditching Jay so suddenly.

"Holy shit!" Dominick closed the door. "How does my hair look?"

"Awful, as usual." Garrett paused the show. "Who is it? Old Grindr date? Mine or yours?"

"As if I would care what any of those goblins thought of me." Dominick ran his fingers through his hair. "Isla's boss is here."

Isla gaped at Dominick. What did he say?

"What?!" Garrett leaped to his feet. "We're going to meet Jayden-James Hancock?!"

An embarrassingly thick burst of relief swept through Isla. "H-he's probably just here to pick up his keys. Let me deal with him."

The last thing she needed was her roommates to make things worse with Jay.

She checked herself in the mirror quickly. It wasn't going to do if Jay saw her looking like a wreck.

He didn't need to pity her any more than he already did.

Finally, she opened the door.

The first thing she noticed was her messenger bag in Jay's hands.

Ugh. He had to have some decency, didn't he? Returning her prized possession. That was going to make totally hating him impossible.

Her gaze eventually turned to Jay's large eyes shaking behind his round spectacles. The eyes that always made her delightfully dizzy.

"Can we talk?" Jay asked.

"Hi, Jayden-James!" Dominick called.

Garrett didn't waste his chance to be equally obnoxious. "You're looking good!"

Isla groaned and grabbed Jay's wrist. She led him to her bedroom, flipping off her roommates in the process.

Months ago, Isla would have been embarrassed to have Jay in her room. It was a broom closet compared to his spacious condo. Where he kept his walls decorated with framed paintings, anime posters covered hers. Her carpet had stains older than her. She only had a twin bed, while he slept in a California king.

Now, she didn't care. All she wanted was to learn the truth from Jay.

Jay set the bag on Isla's bed and leaned against the door. "You have to know that I wasn't even offered the chance to get this fashion line until after we started making headlines on the internet. My mother thought I was doing the campaign for research, and I admittedly didn't do enough to clarify my position to her."

Isla sat down on the bed, rummaging through the bag. Everything was still in there.

"The fashion line doesn't mean anything to me." Jay reached into his pocket. "Not like the campaign does. Not like you do."

"Uh-huh." Isla removed the electronics from the bag and put them in the same bag as the car fobs.

Jay sat down next to Isla. He still had glitter on him from the earlier photo shoot. Great. Now those sparkles would get on her bed. There'd be reminders of Jay in her life forever.

Isla bit her lip. Would she actually ever forget him? She had a closet full of clothes from him and her cherished butterscotch cappuccino had become his favorite.

Jay showed his phone to Isla. He had a conversation with his mother pulled up, time stamped twenty minutes ago.

I'm not doing the fashion line, Jay had said. *I'm focusing on the EFSLRA.*

Confusion washed away the pain festering in Isla.

"What are you trying to pull?" Isla asked. "Why would you give up the fashion line?"

Jay put his phone away. "I'm sorry for my clumsy words, but please just listen to me for a minute."

She nodded. He met her eyes. Gentleness shined in his expression.

"I thought I was nothing but a professional son until I met you." A glow started to brim in Jay's eyes —that determined fire he got around clothes and the EFSLRA. "You showed me I could be literally anything. And if I can do anything to become the one thing I really and truly want to be in life, I will work hard to succeed."

Isla swallowed hard. "And what is it you want to be?"

She didn't know what answer *she* wanted to hear. She only knew that the anticipation for his response made her heart pound harder than it ever had before.

"Yours." Though Jay's voice had grown quieter, his gaze had grown more intense. "I love you. I think I've loved you since the first sip of butterscotch cappuccino. You are the most determined, honest, and inspiring woman I've ever met."

Oh.

That was exactly what her heart wanted to hear.

Isla blinked back her tears.

She had thrown herself into work in order to be a good assistant and help spread the word of student loan reformation. For months, Isla had been so focused on her purpose that she ignored the vibe she felt every time she was around Jay.

She loved him too.

Jay brought his hands to the side of her face. His eyes were also misty. "Oh, Isla, I'm not worth crying over. Do you want to see me ever again? I promise I'll disappear if it means you don't have to cry anymore."

He really loved her, didn't he? He had given up an important place in his family's business for her.

Their campaign had been sincere, hadn't it? Did it have to end? Did *they* have to end?

She didn't know. What she did know was that she couldn't let Jay throw away his career for her.

"You shouldn't give up the fashion line." Isla leaned in to his touch. "You're good at clothes. You shine when you're in your element. I know how important it is to utilize the skills you're good at. Being your assistant has been a dream."

Jay brought his face close to hers. "You're the very best assistant. I'm sorry I didn't tell you sooner I hadn't meant to give you a job. I hope you can trust me when I tell you that hiring you was never a mistake. I'm useless without you."

"I'm sorry I left so suddenly earlier, and I'm sorry

I jumped to conclusions. The idea that I wasn't qualified to be your assistant hit me so strongly back there, and, and…" A sob welled through Isla. "Oh, this is awful."

Jay let go of her and leaned away. "What do you mean?"

Isla sniffled. "I love you, too, but if I tell you my feelings, I can't be your assistant, can I? I'm so terrible. You gave up a clothing line for me, but I'm worried about my job."

"Wait." A sparkling smile sprung to Jay's face. "You love me?"

"Hopelessly," Isla replied without hesitation.

"I don't see why we couldn't make both work." Jay's smile stretched from ear to ear. "As long as our lines of communication are completely honest, of course. No more misunderstandings because I'm clumsy."

Hope swelled through Isla. She rested her hand on the edge of Jay's jaw. "Really?"

Jay drew his face close again. "Please let me kiss you. I have been longing to feel your lips for months."

Oh, how she had very much wanted the same.

Isla closed the gap by kissing the corner of Jay's mouth. Jay turned his head at her invitation, deepening the kiss between them.

Everything about Jay was soft and warm. Isla had

known this from the start. What she didn't know was how soft Jay's fingers could be as they ran down her neck and sides until they found a home at her waist.

She had read many romance novels and experienced many kinds of kisses, but nothing had prepared her for this quiet moment with Jay. Debts, money, status, all of that became a distant memory as Jay's lips melded with hers. All Isla could feel was him.

If she didn't need to breathe, she would have sustained that sweet first kiss all night.

She pulled back enough to catch her breath. Jay gave her all of five seconds before kissing her again, this time harder.

As much as she enjoyed Jay's softness, Isla found she equally enjoyed his hardness.

In between their sixteenth or seventeenth kiss (it was getting difficult to count, especially since Jay's hands had begun roaming to delightfully sensitive places), Isla leaned her forehead against his. "If we're going to be together, does that mean I get to see you in lingerie sometime?"

A low, guttural groan slipped out of Jay. "Don't tease me. I'd love nothing more than to be touched by you while I'm decked in sheer satin."

A delectable image crossed Isla of running her fingertips along Jay's taut stomach and thighs while he rocked a lavender teddy. That one online comment from so long ago came to mind.

Isla kissed Jay, giggling. "If I get to see you in lingerie, I'm going to beg you to raw me, Daddy."

Jay laughed and buried his face in the crook of her neck.

Isla loved how close they were, so warm, so comfortable. As his kisses traveled further south, panic surged through Isla. She grabbed the bag with the electronics.

He stopped. "What are you doing?"

"Checking your schedule," Isla said. "We can't have you missing any appointments."

Jay tossed the bag aside. "You are my only schedule tonight. I thought I lost you once. I'm going to make sure I never lose you."

A soft chuckle rolled out of Isla. "And you said you weren't good at talking."

Tomorrow. Tomorrow, she could go back to her dream job.

Tonight, she had to find out how good his hands and mouth could feel.

WAKING UP WITH AN ARM AROUND ISLA WAS beyond perfection.

Isla stirred as soon as he started stroking her hair. "Good morning. Sorry, I don't have your cappuccino yet."

"Don't you dare apologize." Jay kissed her. "I'd rather start my mornings off like this."

Isla returned the kiss ever so sweetly. Sunshine and wonder flowed through Jay's veins every time she kissed him.

There had been a lot of kissing last night. Kisses, hopes, dreams.

"Been up for a while?" Jay asked.

"Was doing your schedule." Isla shifted to face him. "You have brunch with Teresa at 10:30, which is an hour from now. So you have two hours to kill."

Jay couldn't suppress his laugh. Isla truly knew how things went now.

"What do you want to do?" Isla asked. "Go to Monahan's and get some coffee? Call your mom and tell her you're going to do the fashion line?"

"Great idea." Jay sat up and stretched. "After I get done talking to her, then we're going to plan the next step in our campaign. I'm going to do both the fashion line and keep my support strong for student loan reformation. Oh! We could make it so every percentage of sales from the college student clothes line goes to the EFSLRA."

A beautiful smile unfurled on Isla's face while he spoke.

Yes, he was more than a professional son. Jay was truly capable of everything, as long as he had Isla.

What a wonderful way to start the next part of his life.

ACKNOWLEDGMENTS

"The Blundering Billionaire" wouldn't have been possible without Tamsen Parker reaching out to me about joining the Rogue crew for *Rogue Ever After*. The whole gang welcomed me instantly, something I honestly hadn't been expecting. Their warm, gentle welcome inspired me to write an equally warm, gentle story.

My wonderful critique partners and friends cheered me on through every step of this story's creation and helped me shape it into the gem it is now. Kate Sheeran Swed, Leigh Landry, Stephanie Eding, Maria Z. Medina, and Diana Hurlburt are worth billions to me.

Lastly, I want to thank all the Jays and Islas out there rallying for student loan reformation. Whether you talk among friends, vent online, call your representatives, or attend protests—you are part of the resistance.

CURIOUS ABOUT RIAN GOODWIN?

Check out an excerpt from Rian's book, *How To Be Good*, available 02/02/21!

I get up from my chair and grab someone's phone from them. "Mari, allow me to introduce you to one of my sidekicks—the Internet."

She pulls out her own phone. "I know what it is. I only have two gigs of data I can use each month, though."

"Isn't that a lot?" I ask, handing the phone back to the person I swiped it from.

"Not even. This place doesn't have free Wi-Fi." Mari sighs. "Can't you just tell me what to write?"

"Your teacher will watch this on TV. Won't they know you had, uh, some assistance?"

"Mr. Stanley always tells us we should use our brains to find a solution. You're a solution."

Stanley. What an unfortunate last name. Or first name. I hope he's not one of those "hip" teachers who goes by his first name. He probably is.

He's also probably old. Stuffy. Throws a tantrum when Shakespeare plagiarism theories are brought up.

Definitely not my type. I like guys who don't treat the classics like the be-all and end-all of literature. Give me a hunk reading manga while watching *Magic Mike XXL* at midnight in his sweatpants, please.

"You're putting a lot of faith in someone who hurls meteors into the sun every other day," I tell her.

"You said you'd get me an A." Mari waggles her eyebrows. "Guaranteed."

This girl. She's so funny.

The audience agrees with me when the segment airs the following week. The montage of me in various states of disarray while discussing the play with her is the icing to the sweet, delicious cake that is this video. Mari shines in the segment, more than my shoes. I'm glad her mother was fine with us filming her.

Once the audience's clapping finally dies down, I move to the spot where I do my closing monologue. I can't remove the huge smile plastered on my face.

"Well, Mari, if you're watching, I hope you'll let us know about that A you got. The very handsome and intelligent Super-Rian has been dying to find out."

More cheers from the audience. Our band, The Velvet Fighters, adds to the great atmosphere with their playful jazz. I love this job so much.

We tape at six-thirty in the evening, finish by eight, and either have meetings about the next night's show for a few hours after or just party. I usually go home in a taxi after the East Coast has seen the newest episode.

The natural high running through my blood tonight wears off once I'm on my way home. Like most people, I ruin my good mood by browsing social media.

After the segment aired, Mari publicly messaged

the show's official account on SuddenPic about how she got a D on her paper. A fucking D!

She messaged only thirty minutes ago, but it's already gotten around 5000 'likes.' She allegedly didn't have strong enough evidence to support her essay topic, according to Mr. Stanley.

What the hell does Mr. Stanley know? *The Comedy of Errors* is the worst. If he talked to me in person, he would change his mind. Of course, he might change his mind anyway if he saw me in person. Another perk of being a celebrity—people love to suck up.

My sour mood improves once I realize I have my next segment just waiting to be filmed.

I follow Mari on SuddenPic and wait for her to follow me back. It only takes a couple of minutes. Seriously. It's after two in the morning. What is she still doing up?

She private messages me first. *OMG. Can you believe I got a D?*

No gushing about being followed by the great Rian Goodwin. Okay. My ego is only slightly deflated.

What school do you go to? I ask her. *I want to talk to Mr. Stanley.*

Lol if you're sure you want to. He's not the type to change his mind. He doesn't even believe in extra credit!! T_T

Definitely old. Definitely curmudgeonly. Ugh.

That's okay. I'm great around old people. One of

my more popular taped segments was the time I
served lunch at a retirement home (thank you,
impromptu butterscotch pudding wrestling).

Super-Rian is not giving up on getting that A for
Mari.

I put on the costume again a few days later before
I "fly" into the school at the ungodly hour of seven
AM with Vera and Felicity at my side. First bell is at
8:15. The school administration gave us permission to
film until 7:45, when students start showing up.

Fastest taping ever. I hope we get enough material
to make a full segment out of it.

The principal decked in a bright red blazer and an
excessive amount of makeup, Mrs. Enns, eagerly
escorts me to Mr. Stanley's room. Handwritten
quotes cover his door. I don't have my reading glasses,
but the handwriting is neat with loops.

Mrs. Enns insists I can go on in, but I knock
anyway as I enter. Superheroes aren't rude. Except for
Iron Man. I'm rich, but I'm not Tony Stark wealthy.
Can't get away with being an asshole when I don't
even own a yacht. Not that I want to be *that* self-
conceited.

But I am a tiny bit vain. Not many people have
my work integrity and sheer audacity to go the
distance for a laugh. It takes an honest spine of steel
to prance into an old geezer's classroom while

wearing an outfit that would make Joel Schumacher's Batman blush.

"Mr. Stanley? It is I, Super-Rian!"

But it's not a crotchety elder waiting for me.

A man in his twenties or thirties in a burgundy V-neck cardigan looks up from the book he's reading at his desk. His black beard is cropped close to his face, pairing smartly with his clean cut low fade. There's not a speck of makeup on him—his dark brown skin is naturally flawless.

His gaze lands on me, and I can't handle how gorgeous his intense, dark eyes are behind his glasses. I instead glance at the book he's reading.

Oh my God, it's *Naruto*.

Fuck me.

I'm in front of the hottest guy I've ever seen in my life, and I'm wearing spandex.

ABOUT THE AUTHOR

Chace Verity (she/they) is publishing queer as heck stories with a strong romantic focus, although queer friendships and found families are important too. Chace prefers to write fantasy but dabbles in contemporary and historical fiction as well. An American citizen & Canadian permanent resident, Chace will probably never be able to call a gallon of milk a "four-liter."

For fans of queer contemporary romance...

Team Phison

Team Phison Forever

Just Some Things

The (Virtual) Bodyguard (in Second Chances: A Sapphic Romance Anthology, *available 02/09/21)*

For fans of queer fantasy romance...

My Heart Is Ready (The Absolutes #0.5)

Your Heart Will Grow (The Absolutes #1)

My Heart Is Yours (The Absolutes #1.5)

Your Heart Will Burn (The Absolutes #2)

The Masked Minotaur

Dithered Hearts

For fans of other kinds of queer stories...

Lucky Charm

Hard to Find

Deal with the Demon